S0-BOK-151

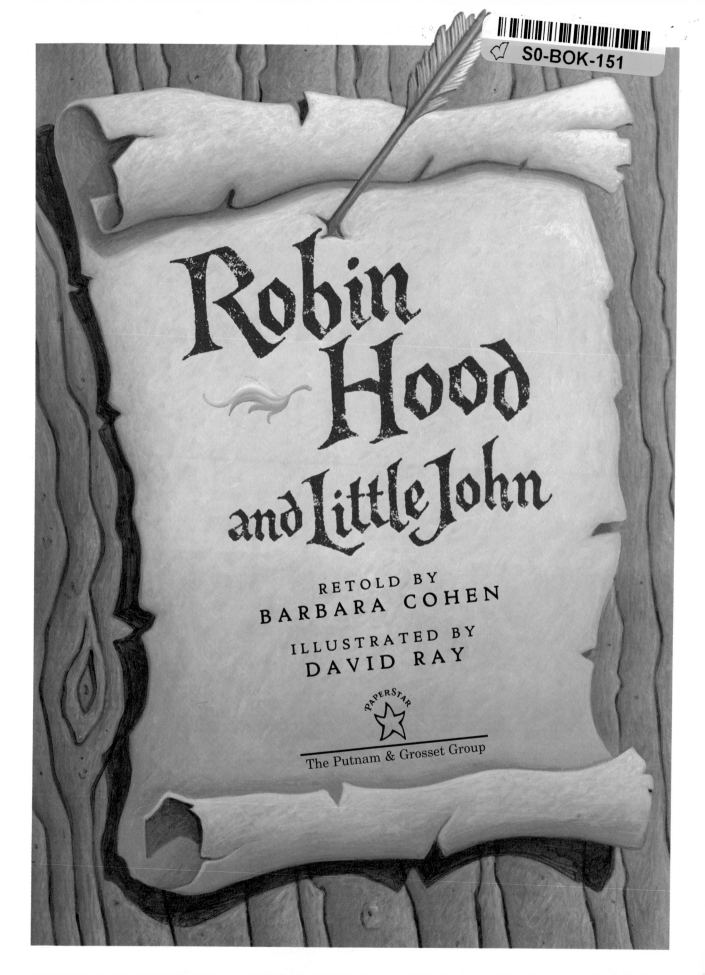

Robin Hood and Little John

RETOLD BY
BARBARA COHEN

ILLUSTRATED BY
DAVID RAY

PAPERSTAR

The Putnam & Grosset Group

For Levi, Jacob, Yasmin, Catriona and Nadav—B.C.

For Patricia Ruth Maher—D.R.

Printed on recycled paper

Text copyright © 1995 by The Estate of Barbara Cohen. Illustrations copyright © 1995 by David Ray.
All rights reserved. This book, or parts thereof, may not be reproduced in any form without
permission in writing from the publisher. A PaperStar Book, published in 1998
by The Putnam & Grosset Group, 200 Madison Avenue, New York, NY 10016.
PaperStar is a registered trademark of The Putnam Berkley Group, Inc.
The PaperStar logo is a trademark of The Putnam Berkley Group, Inc.
Originally published in 1995 by Philomel Books.
Published simultaneously in Canada. Printed in the United States of America.
Book design by Gunta Alexander. The text is set in Cloister.
Library of Congress Cataloging-in-Publication Data
Cohen, Barbara. Robin Hood and Little John / Barbara Cohen; illustrated by David Ray.   p.   cm.
Summary: Recounts the circumstances of the first meeting between Little John and Robin Hood.
1. Robin Hood (Legendary character)—Legends. [1. Robin Hood (Legendary character) 2. Folklore—England.]
I. Ray, David-1940-ill. II. Title.   PZ8.1.C6644Ro   1995   398.2'0941'02—dc20   [E]   94-9944   CIP   AC
ISBN 0-698-11627-5
1   3   5   7   9   10   8   6   4   2

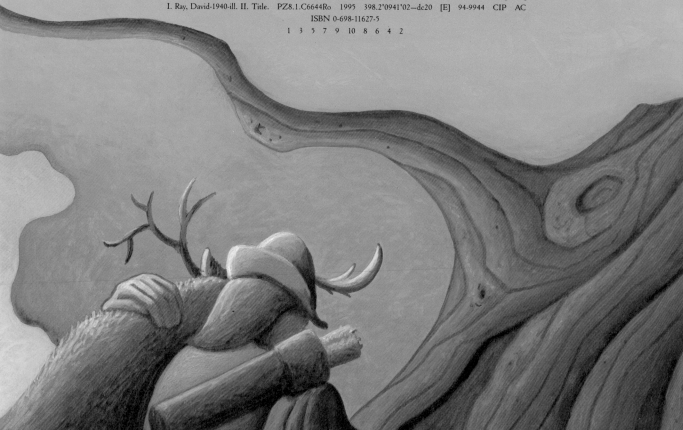

NOTE

"Lytell Johnn" first appears as "Robyn Hode's" right-hand man in "A Gest of Robyn Hode," a long poem probably composed in the mid-to-late fifteenth century, but available to us in a version printed no earlier than the opening decades of the sixteenth century. It seems to be a compilation of several earlier ballads and tales into a more or less coherent ballad epic. One strand of the poem depicts an adventure involving Little John and the Sheriff of Nottingham.

Along with the "Gest," all we have of the medieval Robin is four other ballads: "Robin Hood and the Monk," "Robin Hood and the Potter," "Robin Hood and Guy of Gisborne," and "Robin Hood's Death," none of which can be satisfactorily dated, and all of which exist only in versions written down or printed long after their composition. Modern readers of these ballads are struck by the distance between the Robin Hood they present and the one with which we have been familiar since childhood. Our idea of Robin Hood is the result of a steady accretion of character and incident over the past five centuries, a process that continues into the present.

The ballad "Robin Hood and Little John" was clearly produced by a professional broadside ballad writer for a popular audience to explain how Robin Hood and Little John first met. Probably without an authentic medieval ballad source, its title is first listed in the Stationers Register in 1624. This ballad is the major source of my retelling, which also reflects some of Howard Pyle's imaginative embroidering in *The Merry Adventures of Robin Hood of Great Renown in Nottinghamshire* (Scribner's, 1883), and Walter de la Mare's poem "In Sherwood Far Away."

Of course, I have felt free to add a bit of my own imaginative embroidering, as have all retellers of the Robin Hood stories. The very first balladeer to sing of Robin Hood embroidered whatever reality was the basis of his tale. Indeed, if there was ever a real Robin Hood, his existence is even more doubtful than the real King Arthur's.

For the text of "Robin Hood and Little John" and of the other Robin Hood ballads, along with a thorough discussion of the origins and development of the Robin Hood material, see *Rymes of Robyn Hood: An Introduction to the English Outlaw*, by R. B. Dobson and J. Taylor, University of Pittsburgh Press, 1976.

Barbara Cohen

Robin Hood and his merry men were outlaws. They lived in Sherwood, the king's own forest, and ate the king's own deer. If a fat abbot or rich earl passed their way, they fed him well, but they made him pay equally well for each bite. And they took every last penny out of his purse.

For the deer they poached and the aristocrats they robbed, the Sheriff of Nottingham regarded Robin Hood and his men as nothing more than criminals. It was the great goal of his life to hang Robin from the gallows that stood in front of Nottingham jail.

But the ordinary people of the county—the farmers and dairymaids, blacksmiths and huntsmen—loved Robin Hood. They starved because they had to pay the huge taxes that supported the Sheriff and his master, King John, in luxury. An old

widow who couldn't pay her mortgage or a sick farmer who couldn't feed his family would find a gold piece or a haunch of venison on the doorstep one morning, and know that it had come from their own Robin Hood.

Robin's life was dangerous, but he didn't mind. He loved adventure. And he loved his men—Will Scarlet, Much the Miller's son, Friar Tuck, Will Stutley, and the minstrel Alan-a-Dale. But not one of them was a match for Robin. Not one was his equal.

One fine May morning, Robin Hood said, "Not a single proud knight, not one plump bishop who can pay for the high honor of sharing our dinner has passed through this forest in two whole weeks. And so I'm off. I'm off to look for an adventure. Perhaps I'll meet our old friend the Sheriff."

"We'll come too!" cried Will Stutley.

"Not this time," said Robin. "But if I need you, I'll blow a blast on my horn, and then you'll join me." He picked up his bow and a quiver full of arrows and strode off through the woods.

But the Sheriff of Nottingham was nowhere near Sherwood
Forest that shining May morning. Robin walked for miles and
miles without turning up a single adventure. He was about to
turn back when he came to a stream. The only way to cross
the water was on a narrow bridge made out of a single log.

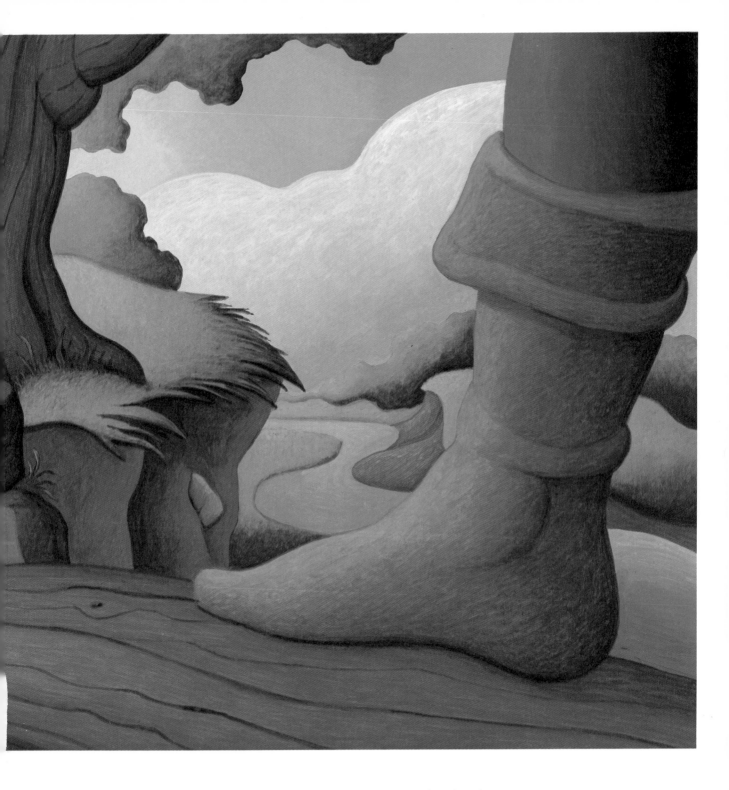

But as Robin Hood put his foot on the bridge, a gigantic fellow stepped out from among the trees on the other side. He was at least seven feet tall, with forearms and thighs as thick as the trunk of an oak. He too placed a foot on the bridge.

"Stand back," said Robin. "Let the better man cross first."

"Do you think you're a better man than I am?" cried the stranger. "Stand back yourself!"

Robin Hood pulled an arrow from his quiver. "If you touch your bowstring," said the giant, "I'll beat your hide into butter!"

"You bray like a donkey!" said Robin Hood. "If I bend my bow, before you can strike a blow there'll be an arrow through your proud heart."

"You talk like a coward," the big man exclaimed. "I have no weapon to fight with except this plain wooden staff."

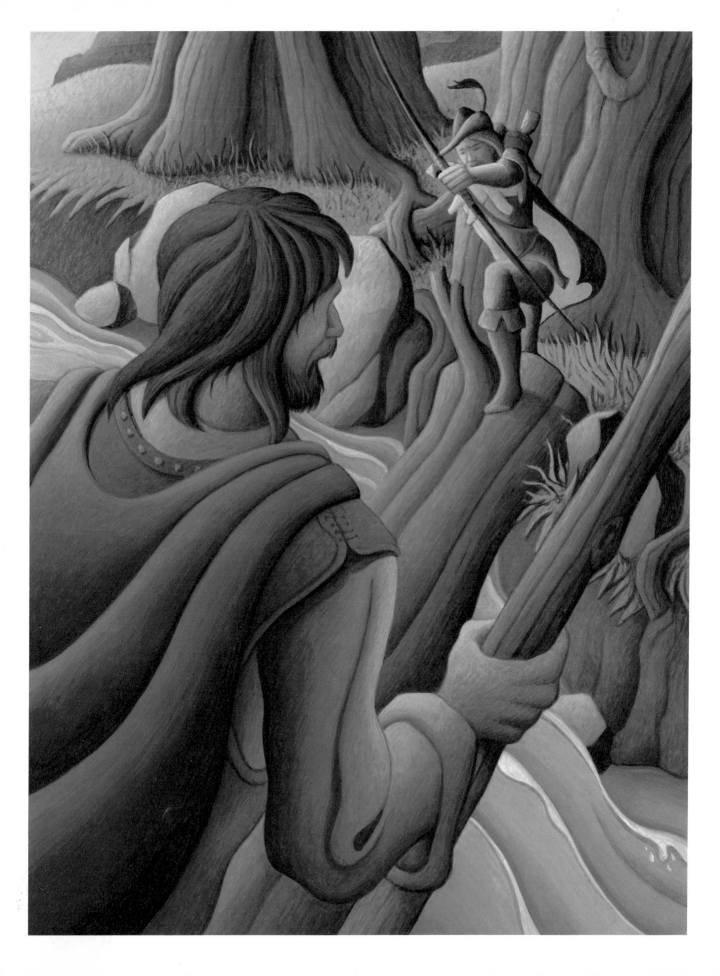

Just as the man was the largest man Robin had ever seen, so his staff was the largest staff. But fair was fair. "Hold!" cried Robin. "No man calls me coward. I'll leave my bow and arrow on the bank and cut myself a stick to fight you with. Then we'll know for sure who's the better man."

"Take your time," said the other. "I'll still be here when you get back."

From an oak tree Robin cut a staff nearly as tall as he was. Then he returned to the log bridge and thrust it forward. "The man who falls into the stream first is no man at all."

"I hope you need a bath," returned the big man, "because you're going to get one, needed or not!"

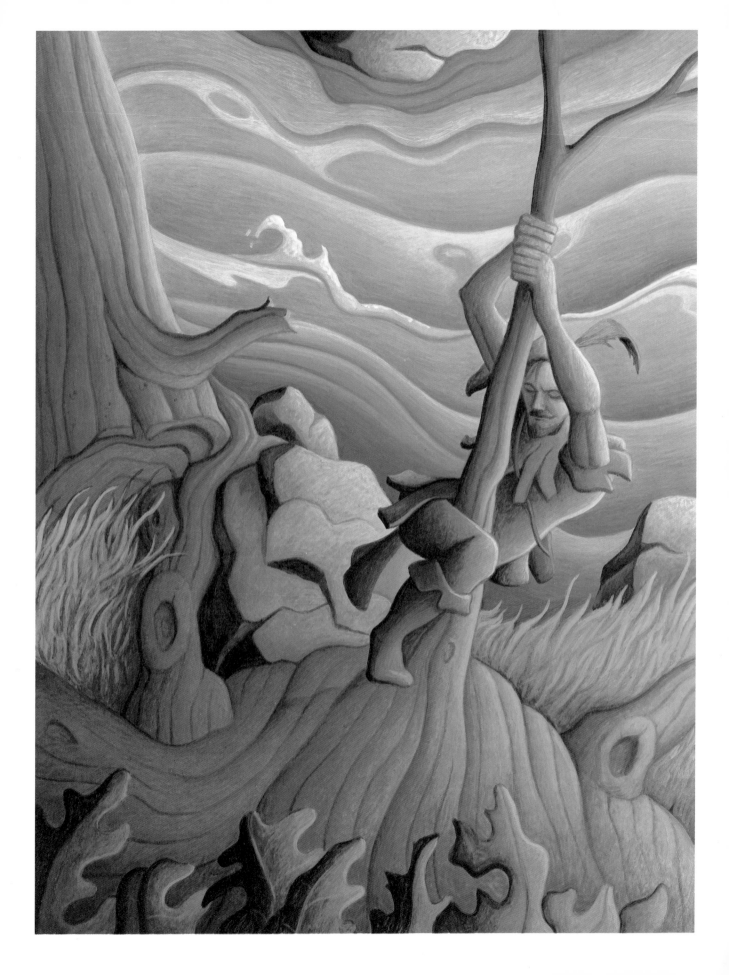

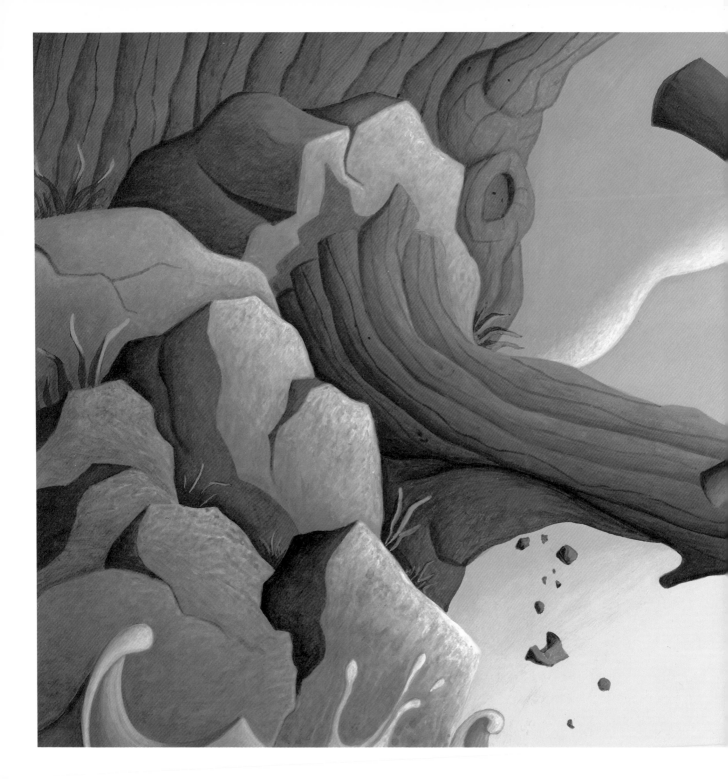

They rushed toward each other. Robin Hood feinted and then struck a blow to the big man's head. But the stranger ducked and returned the blow. With a quick sideways motion, Robin avoided the cudgel.

The two of them stood in the middle of the log bridge

trading blows for an hour, sometimes hitting and sometimes not. But neither would cry "Enough," and neither fell into the stream.

"Such a lusty fighter I never met," thought Robin Hood. "Maybe it's time to sound my horn."

At that moment, the stranger thwacked Robin in the ribs, and Robin tumbled into the stream. The stranger roared with laughter.

Robin swam to shore and scrambled up the bank. "Give me your hand," he said. "I admit it, then. You're as brave as you are big."

"And you," said the stranger, shaking Robin's hand, "you took your beating without a whimper!"

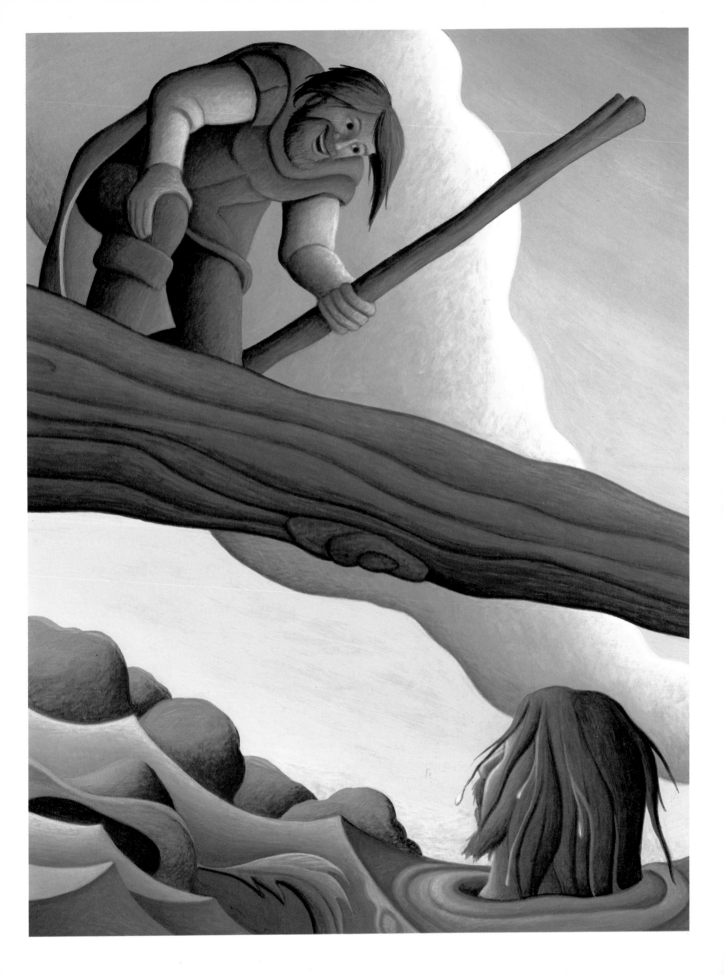

Robin lifted his horn from his belt and blew a great blast. Now it was time. In a moment, half a dozen of his merry men appeared. "Good master," cried Will Stutley, "look at you! You're soaked to the skin."

Robin Hood pointed to the stranger. "This fellow has knocked me into the water, and given me a good thrashing besides."

"What?" shouted Robin's men. Before Robin could say another word, they fell upon the stranger. He struck at them right and left with his staff, so that when he tumbled to the ground, they tumbled with him.

"Stop," Robin ordered, laughing. "Stop! Stop! And why would we harm such a good and brave fellow?"

He reached out his hand and hoisted the enormous stranger to his feet. "Will you join my band? You'll have a suit of Lincoln green, and a share of whatever good luck comes our way."

"Hah!" snorted the stranger. "Not me—unless you can handle a bow and arrow a lot better than you can handle a quarter staff."

Robin shook his head. He'd never met such a fellow. "I can scarcely believe my own ears!" he said. "Still..." He eyed the man long. "I'm going to give in to you as I've never given in to another.

"Cut a piece of white birch bark," he said to his men. "Pin it to an oak tree eighty yards away!

"Borrow a bow from one of my men," said Robin. "We'll see who can handle a bow and arrow."

The stranger chose the strongest oak bow among them all. Then he selected an arrow, set it to the bow, drew the string, and let it fly.

It struck the very center of the birch target and stuck in the tree trunk. The white bark, torn in two, fluttered to the ground.

"Mend that if you can," he said and swaggered.

"I can't mend it," said Robin, surely. "But maybe I can mar it." He picked up his own bow, drew an arrow, and shot it into the air.

It flew in its arc. So true was Robin's aim that his arrow struck the stranger's and broke it into splinters!

"By the rood," cried the giant, "I'll follow any leader who can shoot like that! Who are you?"

"Robin Hood."

"The very man I was seeking! I'll serve you with all my heart."

"Then I've gained a good man today," Robin returned. "What's *your* name?"

"Where I come from, they call me John Little."

"John Little?" said Robin Hood. "John Little? That's no name for a tiny fellow like you. Come with me." Seizing John Little's arm, he plunged into the forest. The rest of the band followed.

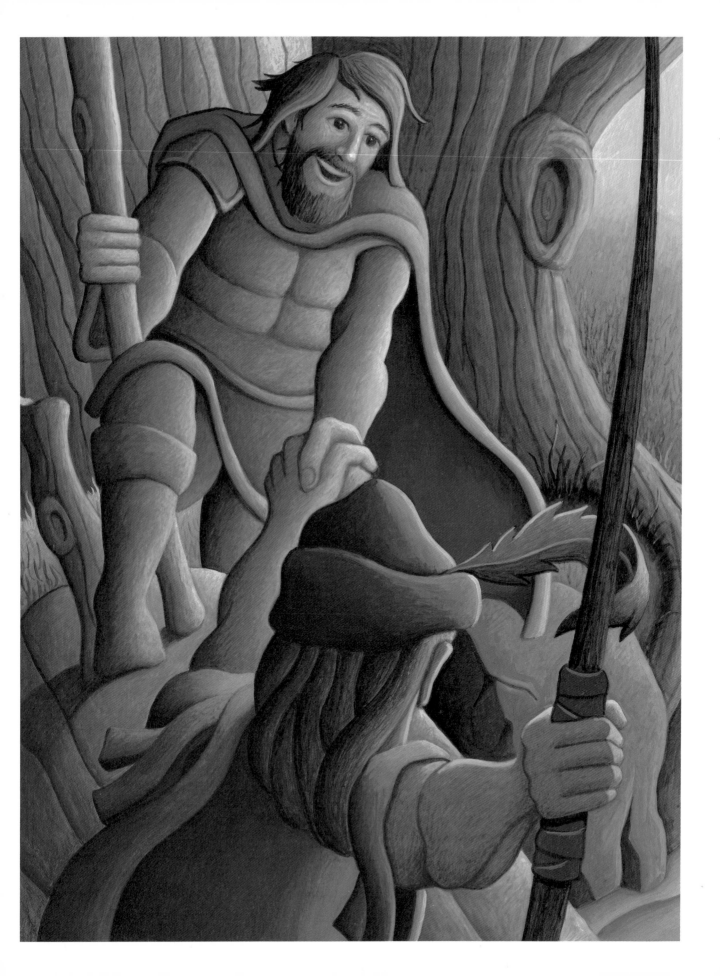

Under the great oak tree where they lived, the outlaws roasted two fat deer and tapped a barrel of ale. While they ate, the newcomer sat at Robin Hood's right hand. Robin made sure of that. After they'd stuffed themselves, Robin Hood filled a pot with ale. He stood up and poured the golden liquid over John Little's head!

"No longer is your name John Little," Robin said so all could hear. "I hereby christen you Little John."

The ale ran into his eyes and mouth. Little John sputtered and coughed. "Little John is my name," he agreed with a great burst of laughter.

Robin dressed Little John in a suit of Lincoln green and gave him a stout bow for his own. "You'll dwell in the greenwood a free man," Robin said. "A free man and my friend."

And so it was that Little John became Robin Hood's best friend and right-hand man. They robbed the rich, they helped the poor, they tricked and taunted the Sheriff of Nottingham as long as they both lived. Together they became so famous that people have sung songs and told stories about them ever since.